ECHOES OF LAUGHTER, ECHOES OF FEAR

ECHOES OF LAUGHTER, ECHOES OF FEAR

KENNETH HAINES

Kenneth Haines
Echoes of Laughter, Echoes of Fear

Published by Spines Publishing Platform
ISBN: 979-8-89569-573-9

CONTENTS

Chapter One

THE FORGOTTEN ENTRANCE

THE OLD SIGN

The old sign loomed over the entrance of the abandoned amusement park, its once-vibrant colors faded and peeling under the relentless grip of time. The letters, once proud and bold, were now barely legible, whispering the name of a place that had once promised joy and laughter. "Wonderland Amusements," it read, a stark contrast to the silence that enveloped the area. Vines snaked through the wrought iron frame, nature reclaiming what humanity had long abandoned. For the group of young teenagers who stumbled upon this forgotten relic, the sign was both a gateway to adventure and a harbinger of secrets waiting to be uncovered.

As the five friends stood before the sign, an unsettling chill danced through the air, mixing with the excitement of exploration. The stories they had heard about the park were filled with mystery and intrigue, tales of laughter that had long since faded into whispers. With each passing moment, the thrill of discovery clashed with an underlying sense of dread. The park, once a beloved destination for families, had become an eerie reminder of the passage of time and the fragility of joy. The children felt an unspoken bond to the place, a connection forged through the shared experiences of their own childhoods, yet they were acutely aware of the shadows that loomed in the corners of their minds.

Venturing further into the park, the group encountered remnants of its vibrant past. Rusting rides stood still, their mechanical joints frozen in time, while faded murals depicted scenes of laughter and delight. Yet, the laughter felt hollow, replaced by the heavy silence that now enveloped the grounds. The juxtaposition of their childhood memories and the eerie present created a sense of unease that clung to them. It was as if the park itself mourned for the joy it once held, and in that sadness, secrets whispered from the shadows, beckoning them to uncover the truth hidden within the crumbling structures.

As they explored deeper, the atmosphere thickened with tension. The wind rustled the leaves, sending a shiver down their spines, while the creaking of the rides echoed like distant laughter, twisted and distorted. The thrill of adventure was entwined with the fear of the unknown, each step drawing them closer to something they could not fully understand. The old sign had promised a world of fun, but now it stood as a sentinel of the park's forgotten history, hinting at darker tales that lurked beneath the surface. The friends found themselves grappling with their own fears, as the line between childhood innocence and the harsh reality of their surroundings began to blur.

In the depths of the park, they stumbled upon hidden corners that revealed fragments of its history: old ticket booths, broken game stalls, and faded photographs of families enjoying their day. Each discovery ignited their curiosity, pulling them deeper into the enigma of Wonderland Amusements. The thrill of unraveling the park's secrets became a quest, yet they could not shake the feeling that they were not alone. The old sign, now a distant memory, had transformed into a symbol of their adventure, a reminder that while laughter echoed in their minds, fear lurked just beyond the shadows, waiting for the moment to reveal its true face.

THE OVERGROWN PATH

The Overgrown Path wound its way through the remnants of what was once a vibrant amusement park, now an eerie shadow of its former self. Nature had reclaimed the land, wrapping rusted rides in thick vines and transforming colorful murals into faded memories. The air was heavy with the scent of damp earth and decay, mingling with the faint echoes of laughter that seemed to linger in the shadows. For the three girls and two boys who stumbled upon this forgotten place, the path was both an invitation and a warning, a gateway to a world where childhood memories collided with the sinister realities of the present.

As they ventured deeper, the remnants of joy became unsettling. The carousel, once a whirlwind of color and music, stood still, its horses frozen in mid-gallop, their chipped paint telling stories of better days. The faint sound of carnival music seemed to drift through the air, an illusion created by the rustling leaves and creaking metal. Each step along the overgrown path was accompanied by a growing sense of dread, as if the very ground beneath them whispered secrets long buried. The thrill of exploration ignited their imaginations, but the silence that enveloped them was heavy, pressing down like a weight, amplifying their fears.

Hidden within the park's twisted structures were remnants of its history that the group began to uncover. They found old ticket stubs, faded photographs, and even a tattered map that hinted at once-secret areas of the park. Each discovery deepened their curiosity but also heightened their anxiety. What had happened here? Why had the laughter faded? The park, once a place of joy, now felt like an enigma wrapped in shadows, with every corner turned revealing more mysteries. The thrill of the unknown beckoned them forward, yet they couldn't shake the feeling that they were not alone.

As the sun began to dip below the horizon, shadows lengthened, and the atmosphere shifted. The park transformed into a different entity, one that seemed to breathe with them. The sounds of nature faded, replaced by an oppressive silence that amplified every creak and rustle. The group felt the weight of their own fears pressing in, each whisper of wind echoing their uncertainties. Memories of laughter now seemed like a cruel joke in the face of the park's eerie present. The juxtaposition of their innocent past with the haunting reality of their surroundings became a psychological battleground, as they grappled with the specters of what once was.

The Overgrown Path led them not only through the ruins of the amusement park but also into the depths of their own fears. With each step, they confronted the shadows of their childhood, the ghosts of laughter now twisted by the remnants of dread. The mysteries hidden within the park's history seemed to intertwine with their own lives, blurring the lines between adventure and terror. As they navigated this landscape of forgotten joy and lurking fear, they realized that the echoes of laughter were not just memories; they were warnings, urging them to uncover the truth before it was too late.

Chapter Two

WHISPERS IN THE WIND

THE FIRST VISIT

The first visit to the abandoned amusement park was marked by an overwhelming sense of anticipation mixed with trepidation that hung heavily in the air. As the five friends approached the rusted gates, their hearts raced with excitement at the thought of exploring the relics of a once-vibrant place filled with laughter and joy. The park, long left to the whims of nature, loomed before them, with vines creeping over broken rides and wildflowers sprouting through cracked pavement. The contrast between their vivid childhood memories of fun and the eerie silence enveloping the park created a chilling atmosphere that sent shivers down their spines.

With each step deeper into the park, the thrill of adventure wrestled with an unsettling feeling of being watched. The sounds of chirping birds and rustling leaves seemed to echo the laughter of children who once played there, but those echoes were now tinged with a haunting quality. The group moved cautiously, their voices dropping to whispers as they passed the remnants of the merry-go-round, its once-bright colors faded and chipped. The sight of the empty teacup ride, swaying slightly in the breeze, stirred a collective memory of dizzying spins and carefree days, yet it now stood as a ghostly reminder of what had been lost.

As they ventured further, the shadows lengthened, and the sun began to dip below the horizon, casting an orange glow that gradually turned to darkness. The thrill of discovery began to be overshadowed by an unsettling awareness of their surroundings. The air grew cooler, and a thick fog rolled in, wrapping itself around the rides and the friends alike. They shared nervous glances, each one feeling the weight of the park's history pressing down upon them, an unspoken understanding that they were intruding on a place that held secrets long buried.

It wasn't long before they stumbled upon a dilapidated ticket booth, its windows shattered and covered in grime. Inside, they found scattered remnants of old tickets and faded posters advertising long-forgotten attractions. The sight stirred a sense of nostalgia, but it also ignited a curiosity about why the park was abandoned in the first place. Whispers of past tragedies and unexplained disappearances floated through their minds, heightening the psychological tension that had begun to envelop them. They gathered around the booth, sharing stories they had heard from older generations, each tale more chilling than the last, adding layers to the enigma surrounding the park.

As darkness settled in, the group found themselves at a crossroads, torn between continuing their exploration and retreating to the safety of the outside world. The laughter they had initially felt gave way to an unsettling quiet that hinted at something lurking just beyond their vision. It was a moment that encapsulated the juxtaposition of their innocent childhood memories and the eerie present they now faced. With hearts pounding and courage waning, they realized that the park was not just an abandoned playground; it was a labyrinth of fear and mystery, beckoning them deeper into its haunting embrace, challenging their understanding of bravery and friendship.

ECHOES OF LAUGHTER

The abandoned amusement park, once a vibrant hub of laughter and joy, now stands as a ghostly remnant of its former self. Overgrown with weeds and shrouded in the shadows of dilapidated rides, it beckons the curious and the brave. For years, the park had been left to the elements, its colorful facades faded and peeling, whispering tales of joy lost to time. The rusting Ferris wheel looms like a sentinel over the landscape, while the remnants of cotton candy stands and game booths speak to the laughter that once filled the air. However, as nature reclaims the space, a more sinister presence lurks beneath the surface, waiting for the unwary.

When three girls and two boys stumbled upon the park, their hearts raced with excitement and trepidation. The thrill of exploration ignited a sense of adventure, reminiscent of childhood fantasies. They envisioned themselves as daring explorers, seeking secrets hidden in the depths of the park's history. As they ventured deeper, the echoes of laughter from their own past mingled with the eerie silence of the present. Each step forward revealed remnants of a life once lived—a forgotten carousel, a cracked clown statue, and faded signs promising joy. Yet, with every discovery, an unsettling feeling crept into their minds, as if the park itself was watching them, holding its breath, waiting for their next move.

As the group delved into the park's mysteries, they began to uncover unsettling stories tied to its history. Whispers of accidents, disappearances, and tragic events hung in the air like a heavy fog. The cheerful memories they once associated with amusement parks turned into shadows of fear that loomed large. The vibrant laughter that echoed in their minds was now met with an uneasy silence, as they realized that the joy once felt within these walls had been tainted by dark secrets. The juxtaposition of their childhood memories and the eerie present became increasingly pronounced, transforming their adventure into a psychological thriller filled with tension and dread.

The atmosphere shifted as twilight descended, cloaking the park in an otherworldly glow. The rustling leaves and distant animal calls replaced the laughter that once reverberated through the grounds. The thrill-seeking teenagers, once buoyed by excitement, now found themselves gripped by an inexplicable fear. They could feel the weight of the park's history pressing down on them, a reminder that they were not alone. Shadows danced in the fading light, and every creak of the old rides echoed like a warning. With each passing moment, the line between past and present blurred, drawing them deeper into the park's haunting narrative.

As they faced the growing terror of the unknown, the group began to realize that their adventure was not just about uncovering secrets but confronting their own fears. The echoes of laughter that had initially lured them in now served as a haunting reminder of the innocence lost. In the depths of the abandoned amusement park, they discovered not only the remnants of joy but also the fragile nature of their own psyche. Together, they would have to navigate not only the physical dangers of the park but also the unseen fears that threatened to consume them, forging a bond that would redefine their understanding of courage and friendship.

Chapter Three

SECRETS BENEATH THE SURFACE

THE ABANDONED RIDES

The abandoned rides of the old amusement park stood as relics of a time long forgotten, their faded colors and rusting metal whispering tales of joy and laughter. Once a vibrant hub of excitement, the park had gradually succumbed to the relentless grasp of nature. Vines snaked through the once-bustling carousel, its painted horses now dulled and chipped, while the Ferris wheel loomed like a giant skeleton against the overcast sky. For the three girls and two boys who stumbled upon this desolate playground, the allure of the past was irresistible, yet an unsettling aura hung heavily in the air, hinting at the secrets hidden beneath the surface.

As the group ventured deeper into the park, they discovered the remnants of what had once been a place of joy. The laughter of children echoed faintly in their minds, mingling with the rustling leaves and the creaking of dilapidated structures. Each ride they encountered told a story, from the merry-go-round that had spun countless dreams to the bumper cars that had hosted friendly collisions. Yet, the thrill of nostalgia was tinged with a sense of foreboding, as if the park itself were a guardian of dark memories, watching their every move. The contrast between the innocent past and the eerie present became increasingly palpable, heightening their awareness of the mysteries that lay in wait.

Exploring the park, they uncovered clues that hinted at its troubled history. Old photographs scattered among the overgrowth revealed smiling faces and sunlit days, yet the occasional newspaper clipping spoke of accidents and unexplained disappearances. The kids felt a chill creeping down their spines as they pieced together the park's legacy. What had happened here to cause such a vibrant space to fall into despair? The children's laughter that once filled the air now seemed replaced by an oppressive silence, punctuated only by the soft rustle of leaves and the distant call of birds, as if nature itself was reclaiming its territory.

As the sun began to set, casting long shadows across the cracked pavement, the atmosphere shifted dramatically. The park transformed from a playground for exploration to a labyrinth of fear. The once-familiar rides took on sinister shapes in the fading light. The group found themselves drawn to the haunted house, its darkened entrance like an open mouth ready to swallow them whole. Each step inside was heavy with anticipation, the air thick with dust and the scent of decay. The echoes of their footsteps seemed to invite a response from the shadows that lurked within, amplifying the tension as they navigated through the remnants of twisted fun house mirrors and creaky floors.

In the heart of the park, they stumbled upon a hidden room, a forgotten control center that held the keys to the park's closure. Old maps and faded blueprints littered the dusty floor, alongside a diary belonging to the park's last operator. Its pages chronicled not only the daily operations but also the chilling events that led to the park's downfall. As they read the final entries, the gravity of the situation sank in. The laughter that once echoed through the rides had been silenced by fear, secrets, and tragedy. In that moment, the abandoned rides became more than just relics of the past; they transformed into a haunting reminder that the echoes of laughter can easily merge with the echoes of fear, leaving behind an atmosphere thick with unanswered questions and lingering dread.

THE HIDDEN MAP

The abandoned amusement park stood silent, overgrown with vines and shrouded in mystery. What was once a vibrant place filled with laughter and joy had become a haunting reminder of forgotten times. Nature had reclaimed the space, with trees growing through the rusted rides and wildflowers blooming in the cracks of the pavement. For the three girls and two boys who stumbled upon this hidden gem, the park was a treasure trove of secrets waiting to be uncovered. As they ventured deeper into the remnants of childhood delight, a sense of unease began to creep in, blending nostalgia with the unsettling presence of the unknown.

The group soon discovered that the park held more than just remnants of its past. Scattered throughout the grounds were peculiar markings and symbols etched into the surfaces of old attractions. These cryptic signs sparked a sense of intrigue among the young explorers. Each symbol seemed to tell a story, a fragment of the park's history waiting to be pieced together. As they followed the trail of hidden messages, the thrill of discovery was intertwined with a growing fear of what lay hidden beneath the surface. The once cheerful echoes of laughter morphed into whispers of caution, urging them to tread carefully in this place where time had stood still.

As they delved deeper into the park, the group began to unravel the chilling history that surrounded the amusement center.

Rumors of strange occurrences and unexplained happenings had circulated for years, tales passed down through generations. Some claimed that the park had been built on haunted grounds, while others spoke of a tragic accident that left a lasting shadow over the once joyful venue. Each revelation added a layer of intensity to their exploration, transforming their adventure into a psychological thriller. The thrill of uncovering secrets soon shifted into a gripping awareness of their isolation, amplifying their fears with every step they took.

The juxtaposition of the park's former glory and its current decay created a surreal atmosphere that weighed heavily on their minds. Memories of carefree childhood visits and joyful laughter were now tinged with an eerie sense of foreboding. The laughter they once associated with the park felt like a distant echo, replaced by the unsettling silence that surrounded them. As the group navigated through the crumbling attractions, they couldn't help but feel the ghosts of their past mingling with the fears of their present. The thrill of adventure was now coupled with the stark realization that some secrets are buried for a reason, and not all memories are meant to be revisited.

In the heart of the park, they stumbled upon an old map, partially obscured by dirt and foliage. This hidden map promised to guide them to the heart of the park's mysteries. However, it also hinted at the darker truths lurking beneath the surface. The thrill of exploration now came with a heavy weight, as the map beckoned them forward, challenging their courage. With the sun setting and shadows lengthening, the group faced a choice: to follow the map's path into the depths of the amusement park, risking the unknown, or to retreat, leaving the mysteries unsolved. The echoes of laughter that once filled the air were now replaced by a palpable tension, as they stood at the crossroads between the innocence of their childhood and the haunting realities of their discovery.

Chapter Four

SHADOWS OF THE PAST

THE LEGEND OF THE PARK

The Legend of the Park tells the tale of an amusement park that once buzzed with laughter and joy, a cherished destination for families and friends. Located on the outskirts of a small town, the park had been home to thrilling rides, vibrant games, and joyous celebrations. However, as time passed and the allure of newer attractions drew visitors away, the park was gradually abandoned. Nature, with its relentless tenacity, began to reclaim the vibrant colors of the park, shrouding it in an eerie silence that contrasted starkly with the memories of its spirited past.

As the years rolled on, whispers of the park's haunted history began to circulate among the town's youth. Stories told of strange occurrences: the sound of laughter echoing through the trees when no one was around, flickering lights that danced across the dilapidated rides, and shadows that seemed to move on their own. For three girls and two boys, the legend of the park became an irresistible invitation to explore the unknown. Driven by curiosity and the thrill of adventure, they set out one summer afternoon to uncover the secrets hidden within the park's overgrown pathways and crumbling structures.

Upon entering the park, the group felt a mix of nostalgia and trepidation. The remnants of the once-bustling attractions stood like ghostly sentinels, their rusted frames entwined with creeping vines. As they wandered deeper, they stumbled upon a carousel, its paint peeling and horses frozen in time, yet somehow still exuding a sense of magic. The air was thick with an unsettling energy, and the sound of the wind through the trees seemed to carry echoes of laughter from a long-lost era. Each step they took felt heavy with the weight of the past, and they couldn't shake the feeling that they were not alone.

As the sun dipped below the horizon, the park transformed into a labyrinth of shadows. The group began to notice peculiarities that heightened their unease. A sudden chill enveloped them, and the rustling leaves seemed to whisper secrets just beyond comprehension. They discovered a hidden path leading to an abandoned fun house, its mirrors cracked and warped, distorting reflections of the friends and their apprehensive expressions. Each room they explored revealed fragments of history: forgotten ticket stubs, faded photographs, and cryptic messages scrawled on the walls, hinting at the darker days that had led to the park's decline.

In the heart of the park, they uncovered a chilling truth that intertwined the past with their present. As they pieced together the stories of joy and sorrow, the line between reality and the supernatural began to blur. The laughter that once echoed through the park transformed into a haunting reminder of what was lost. The legend of the park, steeped in mystery and fear, became a reflection of their own fears, forcing them to confront not only the echoes of the past but also the shadows of their own childhood memories. In the end, the park had become more than just a relic of amusement; it stood as a testament to the fragility of joy and the haunting nature of forgotten dreams.

THE DISAPPEARANCE

The sun dipped low in the sky as the five friends approached the rusted gates of the abandoned amusement park, its once vibrant colors now faded to ghostly hues beneath layers of creeping vines and encroaching foliage. A chill ran through the air, a stark contrast to the warmth of their laughter moments before. The park had long been a place of whispered legends and eerie tales, its history shrouded in mystery. As they stood before the entrance, a sense of foreboding settled over them, mingling with the nostalgia of childhood memories spent in places like this, where joy and thrill were the norm.

Inside the park, remnants of its past life were strewn about like forgotten dreams. The Ferris wheel loomed overhead, its skeletal frame casting elongated shadows across the cracked pavement. Each creak of the rusted metal sounded like a distant echo of the laughter that once filled the air. The group wandered deeper, their footsteps crunching on broken glass and decaying wood, each sound amplifying the tension that hung thick in the air. The innocence of their adventure began to wane as they encountered the unsettling reminders of abandonment—graffiti scrawled with cryptic messages and broken rides that seemed to whisper secrets of the past.

As they explored the warped fun house, distortions in the mirrors reflected not only their physical forms but also the growing unease within them. The laughter that had once been carefree became strained, punctuated by nervous glances and hushed voices. The fun house, once a place of joy, now felt like a labyrinth of fears, with each twisted path leading them further into the unknown. The atmosphere thickened with the weight of anticipation, as if the very walls were holding their breath, waiting for something to emerge from the shadows.

Suddenly, a distant sound shattered the silence—a fleeting glimpse of movement caught in the corner of their eyes. Panic flared among the group, their hearts racing as they turned to one another, searching for reassurance. The thrill of discovery had morphed into an unsettling dread, and the park, now alive with suspicion, seemed to pulse with a life of its own. They soon realized that the park held more than just memories; it harbored secrets that had lain dormant, waiting for the right moment to resurface.

With each step deeper into the park, they uncovered fragments of its dark history—stories of lost children and mysterious disappearances that had plagued the area long before it fell into ruin. The juxtaposition of their youthful exuberance against the backdrop of fear became palpable, intertwining their laughter with the echoes of sorrow. As night fell, shadows lengthened and the park transformed, revealing a haunting beauty that was both enchanting and terrifying. The friends stood at the precipice of an adventure that would forever change their perception of fear, memory, and the lingering echoes of a past they were only just beginning to understand.

Chapter Five

THE DARK RIDE

ENTERING THE HAUNTED HOUSE

As the sun dipped below the horizon, casting long shadows through the overgrown pathways of the abandoned amusement park, the air thickened with a sense of anticipation. The once vibrant colors of the rides, now faded and peeling, hinted at a joyful past that clashed with the eerie silence of the present. A group of five young teenagers—three girls and two boys—stood at the entrance of the haunted house, their hearts racing with a mix of excitement and dread. They had heard whispers of the park's dark history, tales of laughter turned to screams, and secrets buried beneath the rusting attractions.

The haunted house loomed before them, its facade adorned with crumbling brickwork and broken windows that resembled hollow eyes watching their every move. Vines crawled up the walls, reclaiming the structure with a relentless grip, while the wooden door creaked ominously in the breeze, inviting yet foreboding. As they exchanged nervous glances, memories of childhood visits to lively amusement parks flooded their minds. Back then, laughter echoed in the air, but now, a palpable tension replaced the innocence of those days, prompting them to question whether they truly wanted to step inside.

With a collective deep breath, they crossed the threshold into darkness. The air was cool and damp, carrying the faint scent of mildew and decay. The walls were lined with faded posters of long-gone attractions, their cheerful imagery hauntingly juxtaposed against the oppressive atmosphere. Each step deeper into the house revealed more remnants of its past—a broken mirror reflecting distorted images of the group, and a twisted fun house maze that seemed to stretch endlessly. Their childhood memories clashed with the present reality, evoking feelings of nostalgia intertwined with a growing unease.

As they navigated through the dimly lit rooms, strange sounds echoed around them—soft whispers that seemed to beckon them closer, and the distant thud of something unseen. The haunted house, a repository of untold stories and hidden secrets, became a character in its own right, challenging the group to confront their fears. Curiosity mingled with dread, urging them to explore deeper despite the warnings that echoed in their minds. The thrill of the unknown loomed large, pushing them to venture further into the heart of the mystery that surrounded them.

In their quest for discovery, they stumbled upon a hidden chamber, its entrance concealed behind a curtain of cobwebs. The atmosphere thickened as they stepped inside, revealing remnants of the park's forgotten history—a dusty scrapbook filled with photographs of joyous moments, now overshadowed by a dark narrative. The juxtaposition of laughter and fear became palpable, as they realized that the haunted house held not only the echoes of the past but also the potential to unlock the mysteries that had long been buried. In that moment, they understood that their journey was not just about facing their fears, but also about uncovering the truths that lay hidden within the echoes of laughter and the shadows of fear.

STRANGE NOISES

In the heart of the abandoned amusement park, the air was thick with the scent of rust and damp earth, remnants of a once-vibrant playground now surrendered to nature's grasp. As the sun dipped below the horizon, the fading light cast long shadows across the cracked pavement. The rustling of leaves and the distant calls of nocturnal creatures provided a backdrop to the strange noises that echoed through the park. The soundscape was rich and varied, each creak and groan of the dilapidated rides telling a story of forgotten laughter and lingering fear.

The group of young explorers, three girls and two boys, felt the thrill of adventure mixed with an undeniable sense of trepidation. They wandered past the overgrown ticket booths and faded signs advertising joy rides, their hearts pounding with every step. As they approached the old Ferris wheel, a loud clang resonated through the air, causing them to pause. It was a haunting reminder of the park's past, where joy had once reigned supreme. The noise seemed to beckon them closer, a siren call that pulled at their curiosity while igniting their fears.

The park's history was steeped in mysteries, filled with tales that circled like whispers in the wind. Local legends spoke of children who had gone missing, their laughter forever echoing in the empty spaces of the park. The strange noises began to take on a life of their own, morphing into the eerie echoes of those lost souls. Each sound became a puzzle piece in a larger narrative, urging the teenagers to uncover secrets long buried under the layers of foliage and time. The psychological tension heightened, as they grappled with the juxtaposition of their childhood memories of fun and the chilling present reality.

As they ventured deeper into the park, the group discovered a hidden path that led to a dilapidated fun house, its mirrors cracked and warped. Inside, strange noises bounced off the walls, distorting their laughter into something sinister. The atmosphere was thick with anxiety, each creak of the floorboards amplifying their fears. The fun house, once a place of joy, had transformed into a labyrinth of terror where every sound hinted at the presence of something otherworldly. Their imaginations ran wild, each noise feeding into the narrative of dread that enveloped them.

In that moment, the park became more than just an abandoned site; it was a living entity that thrived on their emotions. The strange noises were not merely sounds; they were echoes of laughter intertwined with echoes of fear, a manifestation of the park's deep-rooted history. The teenagers stood at the intersection of innocence and terror, the thrill of discovery battling with the weight of the unknown. The abandoned amusement park, with its eerie ambiance and layered secrets, had woven itself into the fabric of their adventure, leaving them forever changed by the echoes they had encountered.

Chapter Six

THE HIDDEN ROOM

DISCOVERING THE DOOR

The abandoned amusement park stood like a ghost of its former self, swallowed by nature yet echoing the laughter of happier times. Overgrown vines snaked through rusted rides, and trees burst through the cracked pavement, reclaiming the land that once thrived with joy. The air was thick with mystery, a palpable tension that held the five friends—three girls and two boys—on the precipice of adventure. Drawn by whispers of the park's haunted past, they felt a strange mixture of excitement and trepidation. The thrill of discovery tugged at their hearts, urging them to delve deeper into the secrets that lay hidden beneath the layers of decay.

As the group wandered through the park, they stumbled upon a weathered sign that pointed towards the entrance of a forgotten attraction known as "The Hall of Wonders." With its peeling paint and a door that hung crookedly on its hinges, it beckoned them closer. The air grew heavier as they approached, and an inexplicable chill ran down their spines. It was more than just an old door; it was a threshold that separated their carefree childhood memories from the unsettling present. Each of them felt an unspoken connection to the park, as if the echoes of laughter from their past were taunting them to uncover the truth.

Pushing the door open, they were greeted by darkness, the musty smell of dampness filling their lungs. As they stepped inside, their flashlights flickered, illuminating strange murals depicting scenes of joy intertwined with shadows that seemed to dance eerily along the walls. The juxtaposition of bright colors against the dark undertones mirrored their own conflicting emotions—joy tinged with fear. Each heartbeat echoed in the silence, amplifying their sense of isolation. They discovered remnants of carnival games and faded photos, remnants of laughter that now felt like whispers from another time, urging them to uncover the park's buried secrets.

As they ventured deeper, the atmosphere shifted, and a sense of foreboding settled in. Strange noises echoed from the depths of the attraction, sending shivers down their spines. The friends glanced at each other, their expressions a mixture of curiosity and apprehension. The park, once a place of innocent joy, now felt like a labyrinth filled with psychological traps, each twist and turn revealing more about its dark history. They began to piece together stories of lost children and haunted rides, stories that intertwined with their own fears and memories, blurring the lines between reality and imagination.

With the weight of the past pressing in around them, the door became a symbol of their journey—a passage not only into the park but into their own psyches. Each discovery unearthed layers of their childhood, reflecting their fears and the unknown. As they navigated the eerie remnants of the amusement park, they realized that the laughter and fear they experienced were two sides of the same coin, intertwined in a way that made the adventure not just about uncovering secrets but also about confronting their own inner demons. The park, with all its haunting beauty, would forever change their understanding of joy, fear, and the echoes that linger in the spaces between.

THE MESSAGE ON THE WALL

The sun dipped low in the sky, casting long shadows across the overgrown paths of the abandoned amusement park. Weeds and wildflowers burst through cracked pavement, reclaiming the space once filled with laughter and delight. As the five friends wandered deeper into the park, they stumbled upon the remnants of a forgotten era; rusting rides and dilapidated booths stood as silent witnesses to the joy and fear that had once coexisted within the park's vibrant walls. It was here, in this eerie yet nostalgic setting, that they discovered something that would change their afternoon of exploration into a chilling adventure.

The message on the wall was hidden behind a tangle of vines and ivy, almost as if nature itself had tried to shield it from prying eyes. Faded and peeling paint revealed a cryptic phrase, barely legible: "The laughter hides the fear." The words sent shivers down their spines, resonating with an unsettling truth. Each of them felt a sudden heaviness in the air, a reminder that the joy of childhood often coexists with deeper, unspoken fears. What had once been a place of excitement was transformed into a haunting reminder of the fragility of happiness.

Intrigued yet apprehensive, they gathered around the wall, contemplating its meaning. The park had once been a sanctuary of joy, a backdrop for countless childhood memories, but now it loomed as a reminder of something darker. The juxtaposition of their innocent pasts and the eerie present became palpable. The friends began to share their own fears, stories of nightmares and shadows that lingered in the corners of their minds. Each revelation deepened their bond, yet also heightened their awareness of the secrets that lay hidden within the park's history.

As they explored further, echoes of the past whispered through the air. The laughter of children seemed to resonate from the decaying rides, blending with the rustling leaves and the creaking of old metal. It was as if the park itself was alive, holding onto memories that the world had long forgotten. The mystery of the message on the wall loomed larger with every step they took, intertwining their destinies with the forgotten souls of the park. Each new discovery deepened the sense of isolation, amplifying their fears while drawing them closer to the heart of the park's chilling secrets.

With the sinking sun casting an orange hue over the landscape, the group felt the weight of the unknown pressing down on them. The park, once a playground, had become a psychological labyrinth filled with echoes of laughter and whispers of fear. The message on the wall served as both a warning and an invitation, urging them to confront the shadows of their past while navigating the mysteries that surrounded them. In that moment, they understood that the true adventure lay not just in exploring the park but in unraveling the complex tapestry of their own fears and the hidden truths that the park had long kept buried.

Chapter Seven

THE FRAYING BONDS

TENSIONS RISE

As the sun dipped below the horizon, casting long shadows across the abandoned amusement park, the air grew thick with a sense of unease. The rusted rides creaked softly in the evening breeze, their once vibrant colors faded to muted shades reminiscent of childhood laughter now lost to time. The sounds of nature surrounded the park, but they felt different, almost foreboding. The three girls and two boys, drawn together by whispers of the park's secrets, felt a rising tension that wrapped around them like a chilling fog. With each step deeper into the park, the thrill of adventure began to wane, replaced by an unsettling awareness of the mysteries that loomed around them.

As they wandered past the remnants of carnival games and the skeletal remains of a Ferris wheel, the group's camaraderie began to fray. Sarah, with her adventurous spirit, sought to lead the way, while Jake, always the cautious one, voiced his concerns. The boys exchanged glances, their bravado masking an underlying fear that simmered just beneath the surface. Emily and Mia, the two girls, felt the shift in mood but tried to keep the atmosphere light, reminiscing about the laughter and joy they had once associated with similar places. However, the park's eerie silence pressed in on them, amplifying their insecurities and heightening their senses.

The tension escalated when they stumbled upon the old fun house, its warped mirrors and peeling paint a stark reminder of the park's former glory. The entrance loomed like a gaping mouth, inviting yet threatening. As they debated whether to enter, a sudden gust of wind rattled the remnants of the entrance sign, causing them to jump back in alarm. This moment of fear ignited a spark of courage in Sarah, who declared they should explore the fun house, convinced it held answers to the park's hidden past. Jake hesitated, his instincts warning him against venturing further, but the allure of discovery was too strong for the others to resist.

Inside the fun house, the atmosphere shifted dramatically. The mirrors reflected distorted images of the group, warping their familiar faces into grotesque caricatures. Laughter, once a symbol of joy, now echoed eerily within the confines of the house, creating a dissonance that sent shivers down their spines. As they navigated the maze of mirrors, they felt the weight of the park's history pressing heavily upon them. Each turn revealed not just reflections of themselves but shadows of the past—a past filled with unanswered questions and untold stories. The girls clung to each other while the boys exchanged anxious glances, the tension palpable as they sensed an unseen presence watching them.

Emerging from the fun house, the group found themselves at a crossroads, both literally and metaphorically. The park, now cloaked in darkness, seemed to pulse with a life of its own, taunting them with secrets that begged to be uncovered. The thrill of exploration had morphed into a haunting realization that their childhood memories of joy and laughter were being overshadowed by fear and uncertainty. As they huddled together, the bonds of friendship were tested, revealing cracks in their unity. With the night deepening and the shadows growing longer, the question loomed: would they succumb to the fear that threatened to pull them apart, or would they confront the echoes of both laughter and fear that haunted the park?

CONFRONTING FEARS

Each creak of the rides and rustle of leaves seemed to whisper secrets of the past, drawing them deeper into the heart of the park. They were not just explorers of a forgotten place; they were about to confront their deepest fears.

As they wandered through the park, the children found themselves in a world that was both nostalgic and unsettling. Memories of joyful days spent on roller coasters and merry-go-rounds clashed with the reality of decaying structures. The girls recalled birthday parties and carefree summers, while the boys remembered the thrill of racing each other on the wooden paths. Yet, those memories were now tainted by the eerie aura that surrounded them. It was a stark reminder of how time could transform joy into fear, and they felt the weight of those changes pressing down on them as they ventured further into the park.

The first real test of their courage came when they stumbled upon an old fun house, its mirrors cracked and warped, reflecting distorted images of their youthful faces. They hesitated at the entrance, the darkness within beckoning yet intimidating. With a collective deep breath, they decided to enter, determined to face whatever lay inside. As they navigated the maze of mirrors, laughter became tinged with nervousness. Each corner held the potential for a jump scare, whether it was a sudden flicker of light or the eerie sound of glass crunching underfoot. The fun house became a metaphor for their journey—a labyrinth of fears waiting to be confronted.

Deeper into the park, they discovered an old ticket booth that bore the marks of time and neglect. Among the remnants, they found a collection of faded tickets, each one a reminder of joy long past. This discovery sparked conversations about the park's history, revealing tales of accidents and haunting that had turned it into a ghostly relic. The stories fueled their imaginations, transforming their initial curiosity into a palpable fear. The juxtaposition of their innocent memories with the chilling history of the park served to heighten their apprehension, compelling them to grapple with the unknown lurking just beyond their perceptions.

Ultimately, confronting their fears became a crucial part of their adventure. Each laugh masked a shiver of dread, and each step forward was a testament to their bravery. They realized that fear was not merely an obstacle, but a catalyst for growth and understanding. As they faced the shadows of the abandoned amusement park, they discovered that the echoes of laughter from their childhood could coexist with the echoes of fear that surrounded them. By acknowledging both sides of their experience, they learned to embrace the complexity of their emotions, transforming a day of exploration into a profound journey of self-discovery.

Chapter Eight

THE NIGHT OF REVELATIONS

A PLAN TO EXPLORE

The plan to explore the park came about on a chilly autumn afternoon, when the five friends gathered at their favorite spot in the woods. They exchanged stories of the park's past, each tale more thrilling than the last. Rumors of strange occurrences—unexplained sounds, glimpses of figures moving in the shadows, and mysterious lights—added to the park's mystique. Each friend brought their own perspective: some were drawn by the thrill of adventure, while others felt a lingering sadness for the memories that lingered in the air. They decided to venture into the depths of the park, armed with flashlights, a camera, and an old map they found tucked away in an attic.

As they approached the entrance, the overgrown gates creaked ominously, as if warning them to turn back. The atmosphere shifted, and the air grew heavy with anticipation. The dilapidated attractions loomed before them, each telling a story of joy and despair. The merry-go-round, once vibrant with colors, now stood as a ghostly reminder of happier times. The friends felt the weight of history pressing down on them, intertwining their own youthful exuberance with the eerie remnants of the past. They stepped inside, hearts pounding with a mix of excitement and fear, ready to uncover the park's mysteries.

Navigating through the tangled pathways, they stumbled upon forgotten structures—an old ticket booth, a derelict fun house, and a haunted house that seemed to breathe with the chill of the evening air. Each discovery sparked their imaginations, leading them deeper into a world where the lines between childhood memories and the present blurred. As night began to fall, the shadows stretched long, and the park transformed into a realm of psychological intensity. Flickering lights caused them to question their perceptions, and the laughter of the past echoed eerily through the trees, merging with the whispers of the wind.

With every step, the friends sensed the park's hidden secrets beckoning them closer. They shared hushed conversations about the possible stories behind each attraction—what had caused the park's decline, and who might have wandered through its gates before them. The thrill of discovery mingled with an underlying dread, creating a tapestry of emotions that bonded them in ways they never anticipated. As they delved further into the heart of the amusement park, they realized that their exploration was not just about uncovering the past but also about confronting their own fears, revealing the complexities of nostalgia intertwined with the unknown.

UNCOVERING THE TRUTH

As the sun dipped below the horizon, casting long shadows over the remnants of the abandoned amusement park, the air became thick with an almost palpable sense of mystery. The once vibrant laughter of children had faded, leaving behind an unsettling silence that echoed through the rusting rides and overgrown pathways. The park, reclaimed by nature, stood as a haunting reminder of happier times. A group of young teenagers—three girls and two boys—decided to explore its depths, unaware of the eerie secrets that lay hidden within its history. Their adventure would soon transform into a journey of uncovering truths that were better left buried.

Each step they took crunched softly underfoot, the sound drawing their attention to the crumbling structures around them. The Ferris wheel, now a skeletal giant, loomed over them, its once colorful gondolas stripped of paint and life. As they ventured deeper into the park, they stumbled upon a faded map, its corners tattered and yellowed with age. It depicted the park as it once was, revealing areas that had long since fallen into decay. Intrigued, the group began to piece together the park's past, uncovering a series of tragic events that had led to its abandonment. Stories of accidents, disappearances, and a mysterious fire whispered in the wind, blending with the rustling leaves.

The thrill of discovery fueled their curiosity, yet an underlying tension began to simmer among them. As they shared their findings, they couldn't shake the feeling that they were being watched. The juxtaposition of their childhood memories associated with amusement parks—the laughter, the joy—clashed with the unsettling atmosphere that now enveloped them. The girls recalled the stories their parents told of the park's glory days, contrasting sharply with the eerie reality they were facing. Each revelation about the park's dark history amplified their fears, transforming their innocent exploration into something far more sinister.

As night descended, the park took on a life of its own. Shadows danced under the flickering glow of the moonlight, and the sounds of the night creatures merged with the faint echoes of laughter from a time long past. The group found themselves drawn to a dilapidated fun house, its mirrors cracked and walls covered in peeling paint. Inside, the reflections distorted their images, creating a surreal experience that fueled their anxiety. The fun house was not just a relic of childhood amusement; it became a symbol of their fears, forcing them to confront the unknown elements of the park's haunting narrative.

With each secret uncovered, the bond among the friends was tested. They had ventured into this adventure seeking thrill and excitement, but they now faced the psychological weight of what they had learned. The laughter that once echoed through their memories now morphed into echoes of fear, resonating with the terrifying realization that they were not merely observers of the past but players in a story that had yet to unfold. As they stood together, contemplating their next move, they understood that the truth they sought might not only reveal the park's history but also challenge their understanding of friendship, loyalty, and the shadows that linger in the corners of their minds.

Chapter Nine

THE ECHOES RETURN

A HAUNTING PRESENCE

In the heart of the overgrown woods, where sunlight struggled to penetrate the thick canopy, lay an abandoned amusement park, a relic of joyful laughter now haunted by silence. Once a vibrant hub of excitement filled with the laughter of children, the park had succumbed to nature's relentless grip. Rusting rides loomed like skeletal remains, their paint peeling and faded, while tangled vines crept over the cracked concrete pathways. The air was thick with the scent of damp earth and decay, a stark contrast to the carefree memories that lingered in the minds of the three girls and two boys who dared to explore its forgotten corners.

As the group ventured deeper into the park, they felt an inexplicable chill in the air, a sensation that suggested they were not alone. Shadows danced beneath the twisted metal of the Ferris wheel, and the faint sound of distant laughter echoed through the trees, though the source remained elusive. Each step further into the park revealed remnants of its past—colorful signs advertising rides long gone, the faded echoes of music that once filled the air, and the eerie silence that replaced the joyous screams of children. The juxtaposition of their childhood memories and the eerie present created an unsettling atmosphere, prompting the group to question what secrets the park held.

The deeper they explored, the more they uncovered hidden mysteries that only added to the park's haunting presence. Whispers of a tragic accident that led to its closure lingered in the air, tales of lost souls and unfulfilled dreams echoing through the rusted structures. The friends stumbled upon an old ticket booth, where tattered tickets lay strewn about like forgotten dreams. They found a journal, its pages yellowed and fragile, filled with the frantic scrawls of a previous visitor who had sensed something sinister lurking in the shadows. The weight of the past pressed heavily upon them, amplifying their fears and igniting their imaginations.

As twilight descended upon the park, the atmosphere shifted. The vibrant colors of the setting sun cast long, ominous shadows, transforming the once-familiar landscape into a nightmarish scene. Their laughter faded, replaced by nervous glances and whispered fears. The park, once a symbol of joy, now became a psychological battleground, where each creak of a ride and rustle of leaves heightened their anxiety. The line between reality and imagination blurred, and the children found themselves grappling with the essence of fear itself, as the unknown beckoned them deeper into the park's mysteries.

In that moment, they realized that the haunting presence of the park was not merely a collection of ghost stories or local legends. It was a manifestation of their own fears and anxieties, a reflection of the transition from childhood innocence to the complexities of growing up. The echoes of laughter from their past intertwined with the chilling silence of the present, creating a tapestry of emotions that would leave an indelible mark on their lives. The abandoned amusement park stood as a reminder that the past, while filled with joy, could also conceal shadows that whispered of fear, urging them to confront the unknown that lay ahead.

THE POWER OF MEMORIES

The power of memories is a formidable force, shaping our identities and influencing our perceptions of the world around us. In the context of an abandoned amusement park, memories can evoke feelings of joy and nostalgia, but they can also stir up fear and uncertainty. For the three girls and two boys who stumble upon this forgotten place, the remnants of laughter and excitement intertwine with the shadows of the past. As they explore the overgrown pathways and rusted rides, they are not only uncovering physical secrets but also confronting the psychological weight of their memories.

Every corner of the park holds echoes of laughter from countless children who once reveled in the simple joys of rides and games. The faded colors of the carousel and the cracked pavement of the fun house trigger vivid recollections of carefree days spent with friends and family. However, these joyful memories are juxtaposed against the eerie silence that now envelops the park. The absence of laughter creates a haunting atmosphere, prompting the young explorers to confront their own fears and the unsettling reality that places once filled with happiness can become sites of sorrow and decay.

As the group delves deeper into the park's history, they unearth stories that reveal its darker side. Each discovery, whether it's a forgotten ticket booth or a decaying clown figure, serves as a catalyst for their imaginations. Rumors of disappearances and tragedies associated with the park linger like a fog, blending with the nostalgia of their childhood memories. The thrill of uncovering these secrets heightens their sense of adventure, but it also amplifies their anxiety, as they grapple with the idea that the past is not as innocent as they once believed.

The interplay between memory and fear becomes particularly pronounced as the teenagers encounter strange occurrences within the park. Shadows flicker in the corners of their vision, and whispers seem to echo through the empty spaces. These experiences challenge their understanding of reality and compel them to question how much of what they perceive is influenced by their memories. Are they merely recalling the innocent joy of their youth, or are they confronting the buried fears that have resurfaced in this unsettling environment? The tension between these two aspects adds depth to their journey, illustrating how memories can both comfort and haunt.

In the end, the power of memories manifests in the choices the group must make. As they navigate the mysteries hidden within the park, they must decide whether to cling to the joyful echoes of their past or face the unsettling truths that lurk in the shadows. The amusement park, once a symbol of childhood wonder, transforms into a battleground where the innocence of their memories clashes with the chilling reality of the present. This poignant struggle emphasizes that while memories shape who we are, they also hold the potential to reveal our deepest fears, especially in places where the echoes of laughter intertwine with the echoes of fear.

Chapter Ten

THE FINAL SHOWDOWN

FACING THE UNKNOWN

The abandoned amusement park, once a vibrant hub of laughter and joy, now lay shrouded in the embrace of nature's relentless reclamation. Weeds and wildflowers burst through cracked pavement, and rusting rides stood as solemn sentinels of a forgotten time. For the five young adventurers—three girls and two boys—this eerie setting was both a play-ground of memories and a theater of fear. They had grown up hearing tales of the park, a place where dreams had once spun wildly on Ferris wheels and carousel horses, now twisted into haunting silhouettes against the fading light. Their decision to explore this desolate landscape was fueled by curiosity and the thrill of uncovering secrets hidden in the shadows of the past.

As they ventured deeper into the park, the air grew thick with an unsettling silence, occasionally broken by the soft rustle of leaves or the distant creaking of metal. Each step echoed with the ghosts of laughter long gone, and the juxtaposition of their childhood memories with the park's eerie present heightened their senses. The thrill of discovery mingled with an undercurrent of dread, as they stumbled upon remnants of old games, peeling paint, and faded signs promising joy. The thrill-seekers became reluctant explorers, each corner turned revealing not just artifacts of joy, but also the unsettling realization that they were not alone in their exploration.

The atmosphere grew increasingly oppressive as they uncovered layers of the park's history—whispers of accidents, disappearances, and unexplained events that had cast a long shadow over the once-beloved destination. The thrill of their adventure began to morph into something darker as the friends shared stories, each one more chilling than the last. Their imaginations ran wild, painting vivid pictures of the park's past, and as the sun dipped below the horizon, the fear of the unknown crept in. The once inviting shadows transformed into menacing figures, and the playful laughter of their childhood memories faded into echoes of anxiety.

In the heart of the park stood the remnants of the fun house, a maze of mirrors and illusions that seemed to mock their sense of reality. It became a symbol of their growing fear, reflecting not only their physical surroundings but also the psychological turmoil brewing within each of them. As they entered, the laughter that had once filled the space was replaced with an eerie stillness, each reflection twisting their features into grotesque parodies. The fun house challenged their perceptions of safety and familiarity, forcing them to confront the fears that lurked just beneath the surface of their youthful bravado.

Ultimately, "Facing the Unknown" was not just about the physical exploration of an abandoned amusement park; it was a journey into the depths of their own fears and insecurities. In the heart of the park, they confronted the reality that the past could not be easily forgotten, and the memories that once brought them joy now carried an edge of terror. As they emerged from the shadows, the thrill of discovery remained intertwined with the lessons learned about fear, friendship, and the haunting echoes of laughter that lingered in places long forgotten.

THE CHOICE

The abandoned amusement park loomed before the group, its once vibrant colors now dulled by the relentless grip of nature. Vines coiled around rusted rides, and the laughter of children seemed to echo through the air, reminiscent of a time long forgotten. As the three girls and two boys stood at the entrance, a mix of excitement and trepidation washed over them. This was not just a place of fun; it was a canvas painted with memories and shadows, where the past intertwined with the present. The decision to explore the park was not just about curiosity; it was a choice that would lead them into the heart of its mysteries.

As they stepped further inside, the haunting melodies of the carousel mixed with the whispers of the wind, creating an unsettling atmosphere. Each creak of the old rides seemed to beckon them deeper into the park's secrets. They were drawn to the ghostly remnants of childhood joy, yet an underlying fear gnawed at them. The thrill of adventure clashed with the unease of their surroundings. The choice before them was clear: to turn back to safety or to plunge into the unknown. This decision would soon reveal the psychological depths of their fears and the strength of their friendships.

The park held a history shrouded in rumors and half-told tales. Legends spoke of disappearances and strange occurrences that had plagued the amusement park long before its closure. The group felt the weight of these stories as they navigated through the dilapidated attractions, each one a reminder of the laughter that once filled the air. Their imaginations ran wild, transforming innocent memories into vivid nightmares. The juxtaposition of their childhood joy and the eerie present heightened their senses, making every shadow seem alive, every sound a possible threat.

As they ventured deeper, a chilling realization began to surface. The park was not merely a relic of the past; it was a living entity that seemed to respond to their presence. The choice to continue exploring morphed into a battle against their instincts. Fear whispered in their ears, urging them to flee, while curiosity pushed them forward. The psychological thrill of confronting their fears became palpable, binding them together in their shared experience. Each decision they made not only shaped their adventure but also tested the strength of their bonds.

Ultimately, "The Choice" was more than about entering the park; it was about confronting the echoes of laughter that had once filled their lives and the fears that now threatened to consume them. As the sun dipped below the horizon, casting long shadows across the overgrown paths, they realized that their journey was not just a quest for discovery but a profound exploration of their own inner fears and the complexities of growing up. The amusement park, with its secrets and mysteries, would forever alter their understanding of courage, friendship, and the haunting beauty of memories intertwined with fear.

Chapter Eleven

THE AFTERMATH

REFLECTIONS AND RECONCILIATION

As the sun began to dip below the horizon, casting long shadows through the overgrown pathways of the abandoned amusement park, the five friends stood in a moment of silence. The air was thick with the scent of damp earth and decaying wood, a stark reminder of the park's forgotten past. They had stumbled upon this place, a forgotten relic of laughter and joy, now overtaken by nature's relentless embrace. Each corner of the park whispered secrets of its former glory, and yet, there was an unsettling aura that seemed to pulse with every gust of wind. The thrill of discovery danced in the air, but so too did the weight of the unknown.

As they ventured deeper into the park, the remnants of childhood joy became increasingly intertwined with an unsettling eeriness. The rusted rides, once vibrant with laughter, stood motionless, their paint peeling and their structures creaking like ancient bones. The Ferris wheel loomed overhead, a towering giant watching over the friends as they navigated through the remnants of forgotten games and attractions. They could almost hear echoes of the past—the screams of delight from children long gone mixed with the haunting silence that now enveloped the place. Each step forward felt like a step deeper into a story that had been left unfinished.

The exploration took a turn when they stumbled upon a hidden area, overgrown with vines and shrouded in mystery. Here, the air seemed heavier, as if the very ground held onto the park's buried secrets. The group found an old, tattered map that hinted at long-lost attractions and hidden spots. It was a treasure map of sorts, promising adventures yet to be uncovered but also hinting at the darker tales that lingered in the shadows. The thrill of the hunt ignited their imaginations, but as they pieced together the park's history, a sense of dread began to creep in. What had happened here? Who had once called this place home, and why had it been abandoned?

As they delved into the park's lore, the stories they uncovered painted a picture of a vibrant community that had once thrived there. Laughter echoed through the air, and children raced to claim their favorite rides. But with each revelation, they also encountered tales of tragic accidents and lingering spirits. The juxtaposition of these childhood memories against the eerie present created a palpable tension, forcing the friends to confront their own fears. The park became a living entity, a place that held both memories of joy and shadows of sorrow, reflecting the complexities of their own lives.

In the end, the experience in the abandoned amusement park became a journey of reflection and reconciliation for the friends. They learned to navigate their fears, recognizing that the unknown could offer both fright and fascination. As they shared stories and faced the lingering shadows of the past together, they forged a deeper bond with each other and with the memories that the park held. They left the park with a newfound understanding of the delicate balance between joy and fear, laughter and sorrow, and the importance of embracing both as essential parts of their growing selves. The echoes of their adventure would linger long after they stepped beyond the park's gates, a reminder of the mysteries that lie within both the world and themselves.

MOVING FORWARD

The journey of rediscovery often begins with a single step into the unknown, and for the five friends, that step led them into the depths of an abandoned amusement park, long forgotten by the world but alive with the whispers of its past. As they ventured deeper into the park, the echoes of laughter that once filled the air were now replaced by an unsettling silence, interrupted only by the rustle of leaves and the creak of rusting rides. The juxtaposition of their childhood memories of joyous days spent in similar places contrasted sharply with the eerie present they found themselves in. This park, once a sanctuary of fun, now stood as a testament to time and decay, its secrets waiting to be unearthed.

The group was drawn to the remnants of vibrant attractions that had faded into the shadows, their colors muted by the passage of time. The Ferris wheel, now a skeletal structure, loomed over them like a giant guardian of forgotten dreams. As they explored, they stumbled upon remnants of games, stalls, and pathways that told stories of laughter and excitement, now overlaid with an unsettling silence. Each discovery added layers to the park's history, igniting their imaginations and sparking questions that lingered in the air like the scent of damp earth. What had caused the park's demise? What stories lay hidden behind its crumbling facades?

As they delved further into the park, the atmosphere thickened with an unshakable tension. Shadows danced in the corners of their vision, and the weight of history pressed upon their shoulders. The tales of lost children, of laughter turned to screams, and of secrets buried so deep that they threatened to sink the very ground beneath their feet began to surface. The friends found themselves divided between the thrill of exploration and the creeping dread that a darker force might be at play. Each creak of the old rides, each rustle of the trees, seemed to echo their deepest fears, transforming their innocent adventure into a psychological thriller of survival.

The allure of uncovering the park's mysteries grew stronger with each passing moment, compelling them to confront their fears. They began to piece together clues, drawing on the remnants of the park's history and the stories they had heard from locals, each tale more chilling than the last. What had once been a source of joy was now a puzzle shrouded in darkness. The thrill of discovery became intertwined with an instinctual urge to flee, creating a push and pull in their hearts as they weighed the risks against the potential rewards of knowledge. This tension transformed their journey into an exploration of not just the park, but of their own resilience in the face of fear.

In moving forward, the five friends found strength in their unity, relying on each other to navigate the eerie landscape. Their shared laughter, once a simple expression of joy, became a lifeline, echoing against the desolate backdrop of the park. While the shadows of the past threatened to engulf them, it was their bond that illuminated the path ahead. As they ventured deeper, they learned that confronting fear is not just about facing the unknown but also about reclaiming the laughter and memories that make them who they are. In embracing both the echoes of fear and the echoes of laughter, they discovered that moving forward meant not only uncovering the secrets of the park but also reaffirming their friendship and courage in the face of the unsettling.

www.ingramcontent.com/pod-product-compliance
Lightning Source LLC
LaVergne TN
LVHW010505160826
845677LV00012B/2674